My Fellow Unicorns,
All the things that others say that make you "different" or "weird" are *your* magic.
Your life is *your* story to write; and I hope yours is filled with magic.
And to John, what can I neigh?! You're haw-some. Couldn't have done this without you, thanks!
—Jason

IMPRINT
A part of Macmillan Publishing Group, LLC
120 Broadway, New York, NY 10271

ABOUT THIS BOOK
All art for this book was digitally created in Illustrator and Photoshop using a Wacom Cintiq.
The text was set in Apercu, and the display type is Forest Puyehue Family. The book was
edited by John Morgan and designed by Carolyn Bull. The production was supervised
by Raymond Ernesto Colón, and the production editor was Dawn Ryan.

Library of Congress Control Number: 2019941099
ISBN 978-1-250-31132-0 (hardcover)

Our books may be purchased in bulk for promotional, educational, or business use.
Please contact your local bookseller or the Macmillan Corporate and
Premium Sales Department at (800) 221-7945 ext. 5442 or by email
at MacmillanSpecialMarkets@macmillan.com.

Imprint logo designed by Amanda Spielman

First edition, 2020

1 3 5 7 9 10 8 6 4 2

mackids.com

Feel free to take a look, just don't steal this book.
See, it's full of unicorn magic, and that sounds cool, I know . . .
But stealing will awaken Cletus, the world's worst unicorn, to come to your
house and fart the stinkiest rainbow toots in your face—forever!
Unicorns are cool, thieves are just fools!

IT'S OKAY TO BE A UNICORN!

JASON THARP

【Imprint】
MAKE YOUR MARK

NEW YORK

In the quiet town of Hoofington lived
CORNELIUS J. SPARKLESTEED.
He was famous for making incredible hats.

It was almost time for Cornelius's favorite holiday festival: HOOFAPALOOZA. Hoofapalooza was about everything horse-tastic, and it always had a special final performance. Last year, Bonnet pulled a statue of Neighbraham Lincoln across a field. The year before, Clyde stomped the alphabet.

For this year's Hoofapalooza, Mayor Mare called Cornelius to Town Hall for a special request.

"I want the most UN-UNICORNY hat you can make!" the mayor said.

All Cornelius could think to say was, "Sure, Mr. Mayor." He went home to get started.

As Cornelius worked, he thought about how Hoofington's horses were nice to everyhorse . . . except unicorns.

They said lots of mean things about unicorns. Cornelius knew none of it was true, but he never said anything back. And he always kept his BIG SECRET hidden under his hat.

When Mayor Mare picked up his hat, he said, **"WOW, IT LOOKS GREAT!** Your hats are so creative! I'm choosing you to perform the **FINAL SHOW** at Hoofapalooza! I can't wait to see what you do onstage!"

"THAT'S HOOFERRIFIC!" Cornelius said. "Thank you so much, Mr. Mayor! I won't let you down!"

On Monday, Cornelius stopped by his friend
Tilly's doughnut shop.

"Congratulations on being picked for the
Hoofapalooza final show!" Tilly said. "I've been working
on new flavors. What do you think?"

Cornelius took a bite. "Holy hay, these are so yummy! But have you ever thought about even more exciting flavors? Maybe CHOCOLATE HAY FEVER? WOWIE STRAW-STRAWBERRY? SUPER-SOUR GREEN APPLE GRASS?"

Tilly looked thoughtful.

On Tuesday, Cornelius ran into his friend Hablo Horsecasso at Hoofington Art Supply. They both wanted the last tube of sparkle bright blue, so they agreed to share it.

"I need that blue for my mural for Hoofapalooza," Hablo explained. "I feel like it's missing something."

"Have you thought about adding a double rainbow?" Cornelius asked. "No, wait—A TRIPLE RAINBOW!!!"

Hablo looked thoughtful.

On Wednesday, Cornelius galloped to DJ Salad's recording studio to ask for help with the music for his Hoofapalooza performance.

"I'm down with that," DJ Salad said. "Check out this track I just made. Do you think it sounds right?"

"Wow, it's hoof-tastic!" Cornelius said. "But what would it sound like with a WIND CHIME? Or a HARP? Or a little more COWBELL?"

DJ Salad looked thoughtful.

For the rest of the week, Cornelius made his costume for his Hoofapalooza performance.

It had everything he loved: BRIGHT COLORS,
GLITTER, and SPARKLES.

While he worked on his costume, Cornelius tried
not to think about all those mean things Mayor Mare
and the other horses always said about unicorns.

On Sunday, everyhorse was having fun at Hoofapalooza. Yearlings were getting dizzy on the Tilt-A-Wheelbarrow, and ponies were eating way too much fried hay.

But even though he loved the festival,
Cornelius wasn't having fun.

Before his show, Cornelius peeked out from behind the curtains. He noticed Hablo's mural had a QUADRUPLE RAINBOW!

Tilly's doughnuts looked even wilder than anything Cornelius had imagined. CHOCOLATE HAY FEVER STRAW-STRAWBERRY! And DJ Salad's music had wind chimes and harps and cowbells and even a . . . KAZOO?

"OH MY HAY!" Cornelius said.
He felt ready to pull on his costume.

When the music began to play,
Cornelius stepped out onstage.

The curtains parted.

Cornelius put on a prance
to end all prances.

His moves were flawless.

His flow was magical.

He looked haw-some!

As the last music note played, Cornelius pulled off his hat and yelled:

The crowd erupted in CHEERS.
All the horses in Hoofington loved Cornelius.

For the first time, Cornelius felt great for being himself. He realized the things that made him different made him UNIQUE.

Mayor Mare even declared a new Hoofington holiday—**UNICORNINESS DAY**!

Cornelius said to the crowd, "The key to happiness is accepting your **UNICORNINESS**!"

And everyhorse cheered.